Toothw

Written by Jo Windsor

CONTENTS

Rigby

Tooth-Walkers

Walruses live mostly in a world of sea ice and ice floes. They have lumpy, wrinkled bodies, stiff whiskers, and long tusks.

They live together in family groups — herds of bulls, herds of young adults, and herds with cows and calves.

There can be up to 100 walruses in a herd.

glossary

You will meet these words in this book:

<u>blubber</u> — a layer of fat under the hide

<u>bull</u> — a mature male walrus

<u>ice floes</u> — huge sheets of ice that float on the sea

<u>tusks</u> — long, pointed teeth that stick out of the mouth even when it is closed

The Latin name for walrus is "Odobenus," which means toothwalker.

A special body

Many walruses live in cold places.
To keep warm, they have a blanket
of blubber under a tough hide.
This blubber can be
four inches thick.
It helps to protect
the walrus from the
freezing temperatures.

4

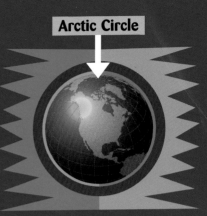

Arctic Circle

Many walruses live near the Arctic Circle.

The Arctic Circle is a very cold place. Temperatures can be as low as −20°F.

walruses spend a lot of their lives in the sea.

They have:
- flippers to help them move through the water
- a streamlined body
- a tough skull

The skull of a walrus is so thick, it is like a crash helmet. It protects the brain when the animal pushes itself up through the ice.

useful tools

Walruses have two ivory tusks.

They use their tusks like arms to haul themselves out of the water. They dig the tusks into the ice and then push up with their flippers.

Some male walruses may use their tusks for fighting. They use them:

- to keep other males away from their females
- to show who is in charge

An adult walrus will use its tusks to strike out at animals that come too close to a calf.

Hunting for food

Walruses dive down to the sea floor and use their stiff whiskers to feel for shellfish. They use their strong lips and tongue to suck out the meat from the shell.

Walruses are like vacuum cleaners of the sea floor. An adult walrus can eat up to 100 lbs. of food each day.

food for walruses

Mussels

Cockles

Clams

Mothers and babies

A baby walrus is called a calf. A calf can be born on land or in the water, and can swim soon after it has been born. The mother can carry the calf in her folded front flippers or let it ride on her back. She is able to keep the baby warm by holding it next to her body with her front flippers, too.

A female walrus feeds her baby for up to two-and-a-half years or more. Sometimes, like other females, she will also feed an orphaned calf.

13

Humongous Heaps

When walruses are "hauled out" of the sea, they like to be together. Even when there is plenty of room on the ice, they gather in humongous heaps next to each other – some on top, some underneath, and some side-by-side. They pile together with their tusks propped up against their neighbor.

index

reports

How to write a report:

Reports record information.

step one

- Choose a topic.
- Make a list of the things you know about the topic.
- Write down the things you need to find out.

Topic:
Toothwalkers (walruses)

What I know:
Walruses live in icy places.
They have tusks.
They have blubber.
They keep together in herds.

Research:
I need to find out:

Where walruses live.
What they look like.
How they get food.
How they keep warm.
How they look after their young.

Interesting facts

step two

- Research the things you need to know.
- You can go to the library, use the Internet, or ask an expert.
- Make notes.

step three

- Organize the information.
- Make some headings.

Hunting for Food

Dive to sea floor.

Use whiskers to feel for shellfish.

Use lips and tongue to suck meat from shell.

Mothers and Babies

Baby walrus called calf - can be born on land or in water and can swim soon after birth.

Mothers carry calf in folded front flippers or on back.

Sometimes babies are fed for up to two-and-a-half years.

step four

Use your notes to write your report. You can use:

Labels

Tables

Graphs

Illustrations

Diagrams

Photographs

Charts

your report could have...

... a contents page

CONTENTS

... an index

index

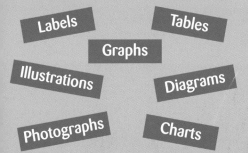

Some reports also have a glossary to explain difficult words.

19

Guide Notes

> **Title: Toothwalkers**
> **Stage:** Fluency (2)
>
> **Text Form:** Informational Report
> **Approach:** Guided Reading
> **Processes:** Thinking Critically, Exploring Language, Processing Information
> **Written and Visual Focus**: Informational Report, Glossary, Illustrative Diagram

THINKING CRITICALLY
(sample questions)

Before Reading – Establishing Prior Knowledge
- What do you know about the walrus?

Visualizing the Text Content
- What might you expect to see in this book?
- What form of writing do you think will be used by the author?

Look at the contents page and index. Encourage the children to think about the information and make predictions about the text content.

After Reading – Interpreting the Text
- What do you think would happen to the sea floor if the walruses did not eat so much?
- What do you think might happen to walruses if they were transported to warmer seas?
- What do you know about the walrus that you didn't know before?
- What things in the book helped you understand the information?
- What questions do you have after reading the text?

EXPLORING LANGUAGE

Terminology
Photograph credits, index, contents page, imprint information, ISBN number

Vocabulary
Clarify: herd, blubber, streamlined, haul, orphaned, propped, ivory, ice floes
Abbreviations: lbs. (pounds), °F (degrees Fahrenheit)
Focus the children's attention on **adjectives, homonyms, antonyms,** and **synonyms** if appropriate.